September 19.

Natalia Loli Cynthia Joey Edelia Miss Byers Victor

This book is dedicated to my dear friend María Amado Byers, and
to the kids who created Little Cowpuncher *newspaper at Redington,*
Baboquívari, Sasco, San Fernando, and Sópori schools.

Henry Holt and Company, LLC, *Publishers since 1866*
115 West 18th Street, New York, New York 10011
www.henryholt.com

Henry Holt is a registered trademark of Henry Holt and Company, LLC
Copyright © 2003 by Joan Sandin. All rights reserved.
Distributed in Canada by H. B. Fenn and Company Ltd.

Library of Congress Cataloging-in-Publication Data
Sandin, Joan. Coyote School news / Joan Sandin.
p.   cm.
Summary: In 1938–1939, fourth-grader Monchi Ramírez and the other students at Coyote School enjoy their new teacher,
have a special Christmas celebration, participate in the Tucson Rodeo Parade, and produce their own school newspaper.
[1. Schools—Fiction. 2. Arizona—Fiction. 3. Mexican Americans—Fiction. 4. Newspapers—Fiction.] I. Title.
PZ7.S217Co 2002   [Fic]—dc21   00-039723

ISBN 0-8050-6558-X / First Edition—2003
Printed in Hong Kong

10 9 8 7 6 5 4 3 2

The artist used pencil, pen, and watercolor to create the illustrations for this book.

JOAN SANDIN

COYOTE SCHOOL
— • NEWS •

Henry Holt and Company • New York

Author's Note

The idea for this book came from two sources: The first was my best friend in high school, María Amado, whose pioneer Mexican family had a town named after them. They had a large old-fashioned ranch halfway between Tucson (where we lived) and the Mexican border. We had great times there as teenagers. María had lived on the ranch when she was little, and she and her sister, older brothers, and cousins had all gone to a school very much like Coyote School.

My second source was a collection of mimeographed newspapers from southern Arizona country schools. *Little Cowpuncher* was the creation of a legendary Arizona teacher, Eulalia Bourne, and her students from 1932 through 1943. Five of those students were María's older brother, her sister, and three of her cousins.

Coyote School is a fictionalized school with fictionalized students, but it was inspired by the *Little Cowpuncher* papers and by conversations with my friend María and former "little cowpunchers." La Fiesta de los Vaqueros, the rodeo and parade, is still held every February in Tucson. And if you want to see what the *Little Cowpuncher* newspapers looked like, you can visit our Web site about them at http://digital.library.arizona.edu/cowpuncher.

Joan Sandin

CONTENTS

Rancho San Isidro

My name is Ramón Ernesto Ramírez, but everybody calls me Monchi. I live on a ranch that my great-grandfather built a long time ago when this land was part of Mexico. That was before the United States bought it and moved the line in 1854. My father has a joke about that. He says my great-grandfather was an *americano*, not because he crossed the line, but because the line crossed him.

In my family we are six kids: me, my big brother Junior, my big sister Natalia, my little tattletale brother Victor, my little sister Loli, and the baby Pili. My *tío* Chaco lives with us too. He is the youngest brother of my father.

The real name of our ranch is Rancho San Isidro, after the patron saint of my great-grandfather, but most of the time everybody calls it the Ramírez Ranch.

On our ranch we have chickens and pigs and cattle and horses. The best are the horses. All the men and boys in the Ramírez family know how to ride and rope. We are a family of *vaqueros*. In the fall and spring we have roundup on our ranch. Many people come to help with the cattle and the horses. Those are the most exciting days of the year, even more exciting than Christmas.

The things I don't like about our ranch are always having to get the wood for the fire, and the long and bumpy ride to school.

My *tío* Chaco drives the school bus.

"It's not fair," I tell him. "We have to get up earlier than all the other kids at Coyote School, and we get home the latest too."

"Don't forget," says my *tío*, "you get first choice of seats."

Ha, ha. By the time the last kid gets in we are all squeezed together like sardines in a can. And the bus is shaking and bumping like it has a flat tire.

"I wish President Roosevelt would do something about these roads," I tell my *tío*.

"Hey, you know how to write English," he says. "Write him a letter."

"Maybe I will," I say.

THE LONG AND BUMPY ROAD TO SCHOOL

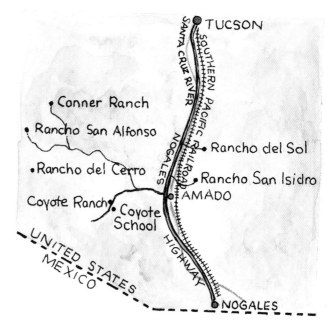

When we leave for school in the morning it is still dark. The bus goes bumping over the dusty road, past the corrals, over the railroad tracks, all the way to the river. Most of the days the river is dry, so it is no problem to drive across it and up to the road on the other side.

This morning the sun was coming up over the mountains when we got to the Nogales Highway. We like the highway because there is no bumping, but we only

get to go as far as the turn-off for Rancho del Sol. That's the dude ranch where Billy lives.

"¡*Mira!*" Natalia said, giggling. "Look! It's Billy and his daddy riding with one of the dudes—*qué* funny!"

Three people were coming toward us. Two of them rode like *vaqueros*. But, *ay caramba*, that other one! He was bumping up and down like a giant jumping bean. Billy says we shouldn't laugh at the dudes, that they come from Back East and that is the way they ride back there, but we kids can't help it.

Next is the really bad road—the one to Rancho San Alfonso—with all the big holes. That's where my cousin Gilbert lives. Gilbert's last name is Pérez, but everybody calls him *Perezoso* because in Spanish it means lazy. Gilbert isn't really lazy, but he hates to get up in the morning and he is never ready.

"Gilbert *Perezoso!*" my *tío* hollers. "¡*Ándale!* ¡*Ándale!* Let's go!"

The very worst bad road is from Gilbert's to the Conner Ranch. But this morning my *tío* Chaco was lucky. Cynthia and Joey were walking to meet us. He didn't have to drive over all the big rocks and holes.

"Edelia is sick again," Cynthia told my *tío*. "Her grandma told me to tell you." Always Edelia is sick. She is eight years old, but still she is in the first grade. She never comes to school enough days to learn to read.

Coyote School

"*Mira, mira,* Monchi," Natalia says, pinching my cheek. "There's your little *novia*."

She means Rosie. I like Rosie, but I hate it when Natalia teases me. Rosie lives at Coyote Ranch, close enough to school that she can walk. Always she waits by the road so she can race the bus.

"*¡Ándale! ¡Ándale!* Hurry up!" we yell at my *tío* Chaco, but every time he lets her win.

Rosie wasn't first today anyway. Lalo and Frankie were. Their horses are standing in the shade of the big mesquite tree.

Yap! Yap! Yap! Always Chipito barks when he sees us, and Miss Byers says, "Hush, Chipito!" Then she smiles and waves at us.

Miss Byers is new this year. Her ranch is a hundred miles from here, in Rattlesnake Canyon, so five days of the week she and Chipito live in the little room behind the school. All of us like Miss Byers, even the big kids, because she is young and nice and fair. We like that she lives on a ranch, and we like her swell ideas:

1. Baseball at recess,
2. The Perfect Attendance Award,
3. *Coyote News.*

13

COYOTE NEWS

All week we have been working on our first *Coyote News*. Natalia made up the name, and Joey drew the coyote. First we looked at some other newspapers: the *Arizona Daily Star*, *Western Livestock Journal*, and *Little Cowpuncher*. That one we liked best because all the stories and pictures were done by kids.

"Monchi," said Loli, "put me cute."

"What?" I said. Sometimes it's not easy to understand my little sister's English.

"Miss Byers says you have to help me put words to my story," she said.

"Okay," I told her. "But I have my own story to do, so hurry up and learn to write."

Loli's story was *muy tonta*, but one thing was good. She remembered how to write all the words I spelled for her.

Even if Victor is my brother I have to say he is a big tattletale—*chismoso*. When Gilbert was writing his story for *Coyote News*, Victor told on him for writing in Spanish. But Miss Byers did not get mad at Gilbert. She smiled at him! And then she said Spanish is a beautiful language that people around here have been speaking for hundreds of years, and that we should be proud we can speak it too!

Ha ha, Victor, you big *chismoso*!

When we finished our stories and pictures, Miss Byers cut a stencil for the mimeograph. Then she printed copies of *Coyote News* for us to take home, and we hung them up on the ceiling to dry the ink. My *tío* Chaco said it looked like laundry day at Coyote School.

Issue Number One   September 15, 1938

COYOTE NEWS

Stories and Pictures by the Students of Coyote School, Pima County, Arizona

Something New at Coyote School

Coyote News was the idea of our teacher, but we write the stories and draw the pictures. The big kids help the little kids...Rosie Garcia, Grade 3

About Coyote School

This year we have 12 kids and all the grades except Grade 5...Billy Mills, Grade 3

We Ride Our Horses to School

The road to Rancho del Cerro is a very big problem for the bus of Mr. Ramirez. For that reason Lalo and I ride our horses to school--16 miles all the days. The year past it was 2,352 miles. We had to put new shoes on the horses 5 times...Frankie Lopez, Grade 6

by Lalo Lopez

The Perfect Attendance

Miss Byers will give a prize to anybody who comes to school all the days, no matter what. The prize is called The Perfect Attendance Award and it is a silver dollar! For me perfect attendance is not easy, but oh boy, I would like to win that silver dollar............Monchi Ramirez, Grade 4

by Cynthia

Chipito

The dog of the teacher is called Chipito. He is very cute. He likes Loli best.....story by Loli Ramirez, Grade 1 with help by Monchi Ramirez, Grade 4

Señor Grandote

Our bus driver ran over a big rattlesnake. We took the skin and gave it to our teacher. She measured him with the yardstick. He was 5 feet and 7 inches! She hung him on the wall next to President Roosevelt. We kids call him Señor Grandote because in Spanish it means Mr. Huge.................Gilbert Perez, Grade 6

Señor Grandote

by Joey Brown

THE CHILES

Every day I am asking my father when we will have roundup. He says I am making him *loco* with my nagging and that first we have to pick *todos los chiles*.

All of us kids are tired of picking the *chiles*. It doesn't matter that we get home late from school, we still have to do it. And then, before the *chiles* dry out, we have to string them to make the *sartas*.

Last night we were taking about 600 pounds of the *chiles* to my *tío* Enrique's ranch. I was in the back of the truck when it hit a big rock. All the heavy sacks fell on me. Oh boy, it hurt so much! But I did not tell my father. He had told me not to ride in the back of the truck, and I was afraid he would be mad.

My hand was still hurting this morning when Miss Byers did Fingernail Inspection.

"Monchi," she said, "what happened to your wrist? It's all black-and-blue and swollen."

16

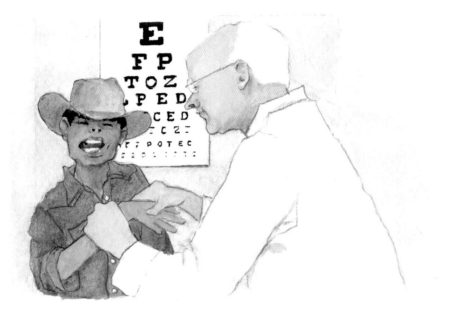

"The *chiles* fell on him," Victor told her. "My father told him not to ride in the back."

"*¡Chismoso!*" I hissed at him.

Miss Byers called my *tío* Chaco over and they had a long talk.

"Back in the bus, *mi'jo*," my *tío* said. "I have to take you to Tucson."

"Tucson!" I said. "Why?"

"You got to see the doctor," he said. So we drove all the way to Tucson to my *tía* Lena's house. At first my aunt was surprised and happy to see us, but then my *tío* told her why we were there.

"Monchi!" my *tía* said. "*¡Pobrecito!*" Then she told my *tío* Chaco to go back with the bus and she would take care of me.

My *tía* took me to the doctor. He moved my hand around. It hurt when he did that.

"I'm afraid the wrist is broken," he told my *tía*. "I need to set it and put it in a cast."

So I got a cast of plaster on my arm, and I had to stay in Tucson. But for me that was no problem! My *tía* felt very sorry for me. She cooked my favorite foods, and I got to pick the stations on her radio. That night Miss Byers called on the telephone to ask about me. She said she would come early Monday morning to drive me to school.

On Sunday my *tía* took me to the Tarzan picture show at the Fox Theater. It was swell! After the show we got ice cream and walked around downtown to look in the windows of the stores. I saw many things I liked. The best was a silver buckle with a hole to put a silver dollar. *¡Ay caramba!* I wish I had a buckle like that.

THE BAD NEWS

Monday morning at school I was a hero. All the kids wanted to write their names on my cast and hear about the doctor and Tarzan and the ice cream and the silver-dollar buckle.

And then Victor said, "Monchi, I think you won't be so happy when I tell you that you missed roundup."

Missed roundup! I looked at Natalia and Loli. They were nodding their heads. ¡Ay caramba! It felt like 600 pounds of *chiles* were falling on me all over again.

The other kids were excited about making black cats and jack-o'-lanterns for the Halloween party. But for me it was hard to cut with one hand, and anyway I was feeling so sorry about missing roundup.

"Cheer up, Monchi," Billy said. "There's always the spring roundup!"

"That's six months from now!" I said.

"Okay then, what are you going to be for the Halloween party?" he asked me.

"I don't know," I said.

"How about Tarzan?" said Billy.

"Tarzan doesn't have a cast," I said.

"He would if he fell swinging from a tree," said Billy.

Issue Number Two   October 14, 1938

COYOTE NEWS

Stories and Pictures by the Students of Coyote School, Pima County, Arizona

Roundup at Rancho del Cerro by Lalo Lopez

The Fall Roundup at Rancho del Cerro

Last week 11 vaqueros came to our ranch to round up the cattle and the horses. The ones we want to sell they drove to the pens at Amado. Then they branded the new calves. When it is roundup Lalo and I never come to school. All the days we help the vaqueros....................Frankie Lopez, Grade 6

Vaquita

I have my own cow. I call her Vaquita. Every morning I milk her before I come to school. She never kicks me. She has a red and white face and a very sweet personality..............................Natalia Ramirez, Grade 8

The Perfect Attendance Report

Lalo and Frankie were absent for roundup. Edelia, Cynthia, Loli, and Gilbert have colds. Rosie stayed home to take care of the baby. Miss Byers said I was not really absent because she had already marked me present before I left to go to the doctor in Tucson.........Monchi Ramirez, Grade 4

Chucata

Miss Byers made me spit out my chucata because she has a rule against chewing gum. But chucata is not really gum. It is sticky and sweet like gum, but it is the sap of the mesquite tree....................Joey Brown, Grade 7

Big News!

Coyote School gets to have a Halloween party with prizes and refreshments! Everybody is invited and that means little brothers and sisters too. We are hoping some of the mothers will bake cakes for our fiesta......Gilbert Perez, Grade 6

Don't forget to wear a costume!

BY Rosie García

THE HALLOWEEN PARTY

The day of the party Miss Byers wrote HAPPY HALLOWEEN on the blackboard with colored chalk. We hung the decorations, and Loli and Cynthia swept the floor. All the way home on the bus we talked about the party.

When I opened the kitchen door I got happy again! My mother was putting little orange-and-yellow corn candies on a beautiful chocolate cake.

It was scary driving back to school that night. We pretended the mesquite branches were long arms reaching out to grab us. Loli got so scared she started to cry, and my mother made us stop. When we got close to the school, we saw two big jack-o'-lantern faces shining in the dark outside.

Miss Byers' desk was covered with cakes, and all the kids had costumes and masks. Everybody was running around screaming, and Chipito was barking at the black cats. *¡Qué barullo!*

seven black cats. Miss Byers was a pumpkin.

The first event was the Grand March. All the kids marched around the room and my *tío* Chaco had to guess who we were. He made us laugh with his bad guesses. He said one of the black cats was Chipito, and that Tarzan was my father, but he knew it was me! We all fooled him and got a candy.

Then we played Pin-the-Tail-on-the-Cat. Miss Byers put a *mascada* over our eyes, so we couldn't see the cat. I pinned my tail on *Señor Grandote*.

After that Miss Byers put some apples in a pail of water. We had to .put our heads in and bite the apples and take them out. It was called Bubbling for Apples. The prize was you got to eat the apple.

Then we roasted marshmallows on a big fire outside and ate the six cakes and drank soda pops and danced. It was a swell *fiesta*! It was very late when it was finished. All the little kids were asleep.

This is what we were:

Me—Tarzan	Edelia—an old woman
Billy—a sheriff	Natalia—an angel
Gilbert—a clown	Frankie—a skeleton
Lalo—a vaquero	Joey—a ghost
Rosie—a black cat	Loli—a black cat
Cynthia—a black cat	Victor—a black cat

Billy's little sister and Rosie's little brothers were black cats too, so we had

COYOTE NEWS

Thanks for the rain!

Stories and Pictures by the Students of Coyote School, Pima County, Arizona

Too Many Black Cats

It was my idea to be a black cat for the party. Loli copied my idea, and so did all of those other copycats....................Victor Ramirez, Grade 2

Gracias for the swell fiesta!

Dia de los Muertos

November 2 is the Day of the Dead. The day before, we go to the cemetery to sweep the graves of our family and put the yellow flowers, pan de muerto, and skull candies the dead ones like. Then we light the candles and we sing and pray for their souls. For Mexican people it is a kind of fiesta...............Rosie Garcia, Grade 3

by Natalia Ramirez

Our Thanksgiving Dinner

Our turkey is thankful for all the extra food my mother is giving him. He doesn't know why she wants him to get so fat......Monchi Ramirez, Grade 4

The Perfect Attendance Report

Only five kids still have perfect attendance. They are me, Natalia, Billy, Victor, and Monchi.....................................Joey Brown, Grade 7

Who Likes the Rain?

The cows and the ranchers like the rain. The cows drink the puddles in the road and eat the high green weeds and get fat. And that is why the ranchers like the rain.................................Gilbert Perez, Grade 6

By Frankie Lopez

Dudes from Back East Don't Like Rain

The dudes at Rancho del Sol are mad. They came out to Arizona for the sunshine, not the rain.....................................Billy Mills, Grade 3

The Thunder

Loli and Chipito don't like the thunder. They hide under Loli's desk. ....story by Loli Ramirez, Grade 1, with help by Monchi Ramirez, Grade 4

THE RAIN AND THE NURSE

For three days it has been raining hard. The river is running fast and deep and wide. It is full of broken fence posts and branches. My *tío* Chaco says only *un loco* would try to cross a river like that, and today he took the back road to the bridge at Amado. We almost got stuck in the mud, and Victor was mad because he had to open and close all the gates in the rain. I couldn't help him because of my cast.

"Did you write to the president about these roads?" my *tío* asked me.

"Not yet," I said.

We couldn't play baseball because of all the rain and lightning and mud. Instead, we danced in our classroom. I had to dance with Natalia. Oh boy! She thinks she is such a swell dancer. She calls me *burro* if I make one mistake. I like to dance with Rosie. She is nice. When we danced at the Halloween party and I stepped on her tail, she just said "meow."

The next day the sun came out and we got a visitor. It was Mrs. Payne, the county nurse. She brought the giant teeth and she brushed them with the *grandote* toothbrush. It was too funny! She gave us the little toothbrushes to take home.

After Mrs. Payne weighed us, she said, "It's a good thing the state has the Food Program again this year. Edelia, Joey, and Cynthia all need to gain weight."

Then it was time for the typhoid shots! When Cynthia saw the needle, she ran out and hid by the arroyo. Of course Victor told on her.

Loli didn't run and hide. "What a brave little girl you are," Mrs. Payne said. But Loli wasn't really brave. She didn't know what a typhoid shot was. When Mrs. Payne stuck her, she bawled like a little calf that had lost its mama.

Issue Number Four   December 15, 1938

COYOTE NEWS

See you again in 1939!

Stories and Pictures by the Students of Coyote School, Pima County, Arizona

Thanksgiving

We did not have our fat turkey for Thanksgiving dinner because Loli felt sorry for him and let him go. La tonta! Our family had to eat beans and tortillas with our pumpkin pie.................Victor Ramirez, Grade 2

¡Feliz Navidad!   Merry Christmas!

by Lalo Lopez

The Christmas Vacation

This is our last issue of Coyote News before the vacation. Most of us have plans for the holidays, like presents and parties. Our family always has a big fiesta on Nochebuena.............Natalia Ramirez, Grade 8

Christmas at Rancho del Sol

At Rancho del Sol we have a big Christmas tree with lots of pretty presents under it. My grandma is coming on the train. We will go see Santa Claus and all the swell decorations in Tucson.........Billy Mills, Grade 3

El Nacimiento

Miss Byers gave each of us a piece of Ivory soap to carve little figures for a nacimiento. Natalia is doing the Baby Jesus. Joey is doing St. Joseph. I am doing a sheep...Gilbert Perez, Grade 6

by Cynthia

Why Is He Called Santa Claus

For Mexican people it is funny that they call him Santa Claus because in Spanish santa, it means a girl saint.............Frankie Lopez, Grade 6

Christmas Wish List

We asked some of the people at Coyote School what they wished for Christmas. Here is what they said:

Natalia "a permanent wave"   Mr. Ramirez "four new tires"
Lalo "leather chaps"   Loli "a little dog like Chipito"
Billy "a toy ranch"   Cynthia "earrings like Loli has"
Miss Byers "a portable radio"   Monchi "a silver dollar buckle"
Gilbert "a rooster to wake me up" (just kidding. Gilbert said "spurs")
....................Natalia Ramirez, Grade 8, and Rosie Garcia, Grade 3

CHRISTMAS

The last day before the vacation, when we were singing "Santa Claus Is Coming to Town," Chipito started to bark like crazy. Somebody very fat in a red suit and a mask opened the door. We all started clapping and whistling and shouting "Santa Claus!"

Santa Claus was wearing my *tío* Chaco's boots, and he had a big bag with candies, gum, apples, oranges, popcorn balls, and peanuts, and they were all for us!

The next day my *tío* Chaco drove Natalia and me to Tucson. He left Natalia at La Hermosa Beauty Salon for her permanent wave, and then he took me to the doctor to cut off my cast. I was happy because my arm was itching like crazy and very hard to scratch.

Under the cast my skin was gray and tickly, but the doctor said it was "tip-top."

Then he said, "Merry Christmas, Ramón," and gave me a cane of candy.

Next we picked up my *tía* Lena. She had many packages with her and the *masa* for the *tamales*. When we drove to La Hermosa, Natalia was waiting outside.

"Natalia!" said my *tía*. "*¡Qué hermosa!*"

"*¡Hermosa!*" What did she mean— "beautiful"? Natalia's hair was very short and curly. But worse than that—it was stinky! We had to ride back to the ranch with all the windows open.

NOCHEBUENA

The next day was very busy. My father and my *tío* Chaco killed a cow and cut the meat in strips. They salted and peppered it and hung it on the fence to dry for the *carne seca*. My mother took the stomach to make the *menudo*. She cooked it all day with corn and onions and cilantro.

Natalia and my *tía* Lena were making the *tamales*. I watched them beat the lard into the fresh *masa* and put some on each *hoja*. Then they added the fillings. For *Nochebuena* they make two kinds of *tamales*—meat with *chile* and beans with raisins. When the *hojas* were filled, my *tía* Lena put them in a big pot to cook them with steam.

For *Nochebuena* we are many people. Some are family I see only at Christmas and roundup and weddings and funerals. The day before *Nochebuena* my cousins from Sonora arrived. Now we could make the *piñata!* Nobody wanted to sit by Natalia because of her stinky hair, so she got mad and said we could do it ourselves. She thinks she's the only one who knows how to make a *piñata*. We all know how.

First we cut the strips of red, white, and green paper. Then we paste them on a big *olla*. When the *piñata* is ready we give it to my mother to fill with the *dulces* she hides in her secret places.

On *Nochebuena*, Junior and my *tío* Chaco hung the *piñata* between two big mesquite trees and we kids lined up to hit it, the littlest ones first. My mother tied a *mascada* over my little brother Pili's eyes and my *tía* Lena turned him around and around. She gave him the stick and pointed him toward the *piñata*. My *tío* Chaco and Junior made it easy for him. They did not jerk on the rope when he swung.

"*¡Dále! ¡Dále!*" we were yelling, but Pili never came close. None of the little kids could hit it. Then it was Loli's turn.

BAM.

Some peanuts fell out. Gilbert and I dived to get them. One by one, the other kids tried and missed. Then it was Natalia's turn. She took a good swing and— *BAM*.

The *piñata* broke open, and all the kids were in the dirt, screaming and laughing and picking up gum and nuts and oranges and candies.

Just before midnight we got into my *tío* Chaco's bus and my father's pickup to go to the Mass at Amado. When we got home my mother and my *tías* put out the *tamales* and *menudo* and *tortillas* and the cakes and coffee and the other drinks. We had music and dancing. Nobody told us we had to go to bed.

Sometime in the night Santa Claus came and gave us our presents, everybody except Natalia. She already had her stinky wave. Junior got a pair of spurs, Victor got a big red top, and Loli got a little toy dog that looks like Chipito. But I got the best present. It was a silver-dollar buckle, the one I had seen with my *tía* Lena in Tucson. It doesn't have a dollar yet, only a hole, but when I win the Perfect Attendance I will put my silver dollar in that hole.

Issue Number Five

COYOTE NEWS

January 12, 1939

Happy New Year!

Stories and Pictures by the Students of Coyote School, Pima County, Arizona

Miss Byers' Radio

Miss Byers brought her new radio to school. It has a big battery, so it doesn't matter that Coyote School has no electricity. We got to hear President Roosevelt's speech to the Congress. He told them to be prepared for war. Then he said, "Happy New Year."........Monchi Ramirez, Grade 4

Our President

waw

by Joey Brown

Our President's Voice

None of us kids had heard the President's voice before. When he said "war" it sounded like "waw." We were all laughing because we never heard anybody who talked like that, but Billy said some of the dudes do............Rosie Garcia, Grade 3

Some Noisy Children

When the President was talking, Loli was noisy. Miss Byers gave her peanuts to make her quiet. I was quiet without the peanuts...Victor, Grade 2

Yap!

By Frankie Lopez

Music on the Radio

We got to listen to the music on Miss Byers' radio. She has many stations, but I liked best to hear the one with the rancheras..........Gilbert Perez, Grade 6

No Earrings for Christmas

Santa Claus didn't bring me any earrings. Loli says it's because he knows that I don't have any holes in my ears like she does......Cynthia Brown, Grade 2

The Perfect Attendance Report

Miss Byers says Santa Claus must have given some of our kids the flu and chicken pox for Christmas. The only kids who still have perfect attendance are Natalia, Monchi, Victor, and me.........Billy Mills, Grade 3

La Fiesta de los Vaqueros Rodeo Parade

We are so excited because Miss Byers just told us something wonderful. Our school gets to be in the Tucson Rodeo Parade!...Natalia Ramirez, Grade 8

LA FIESTA DE LOS VAQUEROS

We were so excited when Miss Byers told us that Coyote School gets to be in the big Rodeo Parade in Tucson—La Fiesta de los Vaqueros.

"Oh boy! We can ride our horses and do roping tricks!" I said. But Miss Byers said no, a float would be better, and she's the boss. So we are building a *ramada* for our float, and we will cook a real Mexican *comida* and sing *rancheras*. Our mothers are sewing fancy *vaquero* shirts for us to wear.

The day before the parade my *tío* Chaco cut the boys' hair. Then we tried on our shirts. Miss Byers told my mother they were *camisas muy hermosas*. My mother was surprised that Miss Byers could say it in Spanish.

Of course all the families wanted to see their kids in the parade, so we were thirty-eight people going to Tucson.

Our family slept at my *tía* Lena's house. Natalia, my mother, and my *tía* got up early to make the *bolas* for the *tortillas*. Then they woke the rest of us. We put on our new shirts and drove to the starting lot.

"We have only two hours to set up the *ramada*," Miss Byers said. "¡Ándale! Keep clean and try not to get distracted."

We worked fast, but it was very hard not to be distracted by the other floats and the fine horses and the marching bands.

My *tío* Chaco made a little fire in some sand on the floor of the wagon. He put a *comal* on the fire to cook the *tortillas*. Rosie's mother came in their pickup with a big pot of *frijoles con queso*. Miss Byers gave us soda pops of different colors. It was time to take our places. The parade was starting!

"*¡Ándale! ¡Ándale!*" my *tío* Chaco shouted.

He slapped the reins, and our float moved out onto West Congress Street.

There were people everywhere! They were hanging out the windows and standing on top of the houses. I never knew there were so many people in all the world, and they were all looking at us!

Natalia and Rosie each took a round *bola* and started to make the *tortillas*.

"Sing!" Miss Byers told us. "Sing!"

We sang. But the school band behind us

with *frijoles*. The rest of us were eating them. We were all singing. When we passed in front of the judges our float hit a big bump and Victor fell in the *frijoles*.

After the parade we got to go to the Tucson rodeo. *¡Ay caramba!* It was such a big, exciting show. Some of the *vaqueros* were from the ranches around here, but some came from far away.

For me, the best event was the steer roping. I liked to see the steers exploding from the chutes like firecrackers and the cowboys racing after them on their horses to rope them and throw them down and tie them. We boys know how to rope and tie, but we are not as fast as the rodeo *vaqueros*.

"*¡Mira!*" my *tío* Chaco shouted the next morning. "There's a picture of all you kids in the *Arizona Daily Star!*"

was playing so loud the people couldn't hear our *rancheras*. It didn't matter. Everybody was clapping and yelling, "Hey, kids, give us some *tortillas!*"

A man pointed a big camera at us. "Say cheese!" he cried.

"*Queso*," Gilbert said, and everybody laughed and clapped.

The whole time Natalia and Rosie were patting out the *tortillas*. Miss Byers was cooking them on the *comal* and filling them

COYOTE NEWS

Stories and Pictures by the Students of Coyote School, Pima County, Arizona

Coyote School Wins!

I think the judges didn't care that nobody could hear our rancheras because Coyote School won the trophy for Best County School! I think it was because of our cooking. Everybody was crazy for our tortillas!...
Natalia Ramirez, Grade 8

The Tortillas

Natalia and I made the tortillas. Natalia's were grandotes! They hung on her arm like big dish towels. Mine were little ones with many holes....
...Rosie Garcia, Grade 3

Our Trophy! by Joey Brown

La Fiesta de Los Vaqueros Parade 1939 BEST ENTRY county School awarded to COYOTE SCHOOL Pima County

The Soda Pops

Miss Byers gave all the kids soda pops to drink in the parade. She told us to take little sips so they would last all the parade, but Gilbert drank all of his in one big gulp and then he tried to take mine....
..Victor Ramirez, Grade 2

100 Percent

We were the only school that all of their kids were in the parade...Lalo Lopez, Gr. 8

A Bad Thing about the Parade

We didn't get to watch the parade because we were in it........Joey Brown, Grade 7

Racing the Horses

I would rather like to race the horses than ride the broncos because the broncos are too wild. And it is easier to race at the rodeo than at our ranch where there are holes and cactus to fall in...Monchi Ramirez, Grade 4

By Frankie Lopez

The Rodeo Clown

What I liked best was the funny clown. A little dog jumped out of his pants.
..story by Loli Ramirez, Grade 1
help from Monchi Ramirez, Grade 4

Rodeo Clowns Are More than Just Funny

A rodeo clown can save a cowboy's life. When a cowboy falls off, the clown does funny things to make the bull look away....Billy Mills, Grade 3

Oh! Please look the other way!

by Lalo Lopez

THE PICTURES AND THE LETTERS

For Art we got to do pictures of the rodeo. As soon as we opened the paints we heard the flies buzzing.

"¡Las moscas!" Rosie cried. "Quick! Close the windows."

Too late. Those mean flies were all over our paints and our pictures. They like the red best. They eat it! They walked on Rosie's rodeo clown and ate his red nose.

"Watch out for your hair," I told Billy. "These *moscas* are crazy for red."

Finally Miss Byers said we would have to give up on painting. "Anyway," she said, "we need to write some letters."

March 8, 1939

Las Moras School
Dear students,
   Coyote School has a baseball team. Would you like to come and play a game with us?
                Sincerely,
                the "Coyotes"

March 8, 1939

Rodeo Parade Committee
Dear Sirs:
   Thank you for the beautiful silver trophy. We liked being in the famous "La Fiesta de los Vaqueros" Parade and watching the exciting rodeo.
                Yours truly,
                Coyote School

Then Miss Byers told us to write our own letter. Who could I write to? I chewed on my pencil and looked up at the picture of President Roosevelt. President Roosevelt! What was my *tío* Chaco always telling me?

March 8, 1939

Dear President Roosevelt:

   Our teacher told us about some good things you are doing for our country. Maybe you don't know because you live far away in Washington D.C. but out here in southern Arizona we have very bad roads. Could you please do something to make them better?
                Your true friend,
                Ramón Ramírez
                U.S. citizen

THE BASEBALL GAME

The Wildcats answered our letter. They want to play a baseball game with us. The Coyotes are not very good, but we don't think the Wildcats are either.

Yesterday the Coyotes worked very hard to clean up the field behind the school. We tied an old gate to Miss Byers' car, and all the big boys stood on it while she drove many times across the field to drag away the dry weeds and stickers. It cost a lot of gas, but Miss Byers said it was worth every penny. Then we put old blocks of cattle salt for the bases and made the lines with ashes. *¡Qué campo magnífico!*

But today we were so angry with the *vaqueros* from Coyote Ranch! They had let the cattle out into our new *campo*, and the cows had walked all over our lines and licked off the bases. We had to do it all over again. We were so hot and tired it was easy for the Wildcats to beat us.

34

COYOTE NEWS

"We lost"

Stories and Pictures by the Students of Coyote School, Pima County, Arizona

Las Moras Are Bad Sports

Friday we played baseball with Las Moras. We were polite and good sports. We let them hit first because they were the visitors. We didn't say bad words in Spanish like they did. ....Victor Ramirez, Grade 2

by Lalo Lopez

The Arizona State Spelling Bee

We have some good spellers at Coyote School, but we can't send them to the State Spelling Bee in Phoenix because it is only for fifth graders and Coyote School has no Grade 5 this year...........Billy Mills, Grade 3

The Government Supplement Food Program

Every day Miss Byers makes hot cocoa and sandwiches for Edelia, Joey, and Cynthia. We other kids only get to smell it.....Gilbert Perez, Grade 6

Loli Gives Us a Big Surprise

Loli wrote a story for Coyote News all by herself. When Miss Byers asked her when she learned to write, she just said, "I don't know. I just do it."...Monchi Ramirez, Grade 4

Loli's Story

My tooth fell out. I hope I get 10 cents for it......Loli Ramirez, Grade 1

The Truth about Loli's Story

Loli learned to write because she took Miss Byers' spelling cards. She did not ask permission. She just hid them in her lunch box. I saw when she was looking at them on the bus.................Victor Ramirez, Grade 2

Vaquita

"I miss my mama" -- Pobrecito

By Rosie Garcia

I am so sad about my sweet cow, Vaquita. She walked out on the railroad tracks behind our house. The train to Nogales ran into her and broke her legs. Poor Vaquita! My father had to shoot her. Now her little calf has no mama. We have to feed him with Pili's baby bottle..............Natalia Ramirez, Grade 8

Easter Is Coming!

My mother is going to color some eggs and hide them in the alfalfa for Easter. She is sewing me a yellow dress. We will have a mass in the church because the priest from Nogales is coming......Rosie Garcia, Grade 3

Issue Number Eight   April 14, 1939

COYOTE NEWS

Stories and Pictures by the Students of Coyote School, Pima County, Arizona

by Eduardo (Lalo) Lopez

Miss Byers Hates Roundup

Miss Byers says roundup distracts us from our schoolwork and she is right. We kids are crazy about the horses running and the vaqueros swearing and the calves bawling. We even love the dust........Gilbert Perez, Grade 6

Roundup at Coyote Ranch

My ranch is so close to the school we can hear the spring roundup, todo el barullo! My father says tomorrow they will brand the calves. We hope Miss Byers will let us watch them at recess......Rosie Garcia, Grade 3

No More Roundup!

At recess we played roundup. All the big boys had ropes so they got to be the vaqueros. I had to be a calf. Lalo chased me and threw a lasso over my head. I fell down and hurt my knee. When I told Miss Byers she said, "No more roundup!"...........................Victor Ramirez, Grade 2

The Easter Party at Rancho del Sol

First we had an Easter Egg Hunt. Then the Easter Bunny came and gave the dudes baskets full of candy eggs, but Mrs. Bean gave me something even better. It's a big sugar egg with a little window. You can look inside and see some fuzzy yellow chicks. I brought it to school to show Miss Byers and all the kids.......Billy Mills, Grade 3

HAPPY EASTER BILLY

By Frankie Lopez

The Perfect Attendance Report

Natalia is taking care of Pili because our mother is sick. Last month Billy had the mumps. I'm glad I had it last year. The only kids who still have perfect attendance are me and Victor...........Monchi Ramirez, Grade 4

Edelia "before"

The Supplemental Food Program

I like the cocoa and the sandwiches. I have gain 8 pounds. I am learning to read the teacher's cards...Edelia Ortiz, Grade 1 with help from Monchi Ramirez, Grade 4

Edelia "after"

by Cynthia

Waiting for Roundup

My big brother Junior and I have been riding with my father to find the cows that are skinny or sick with pinkeye or worms. We give them extra feed or medicine before the new calves are born.

Gilbert and Joey and I are braiding *cabestros* on the bus. We braid them from sixteen strands of horse hair. I am making a short one for tying the calves at roundup. The long ones are for the horses that are *broncos*. Junior taught me how to make the *cabestros* fat as a thumb and very strong. Not even the wildest *broncos* can break them.

"When are we going to have roundup?" I asked my *tío* Chaco.

"Monchi, you have asked me that ten thousand times," he said. "You know that first we must fix all the fences."

"But we are the last ranch to have roundup," I told him. "And this waiting is making me *loco*."

Then one day, as we crossed the river coming home from school, I saw a big cloud of dust and heard the bawling of the cattle and the thunder of horses running, *todo el barullo*.

"They are here!" I yelled. "The *vaqueros* are here!"

ROUNDUP!

The *vaqueros* were hollering, "¡Ándale! ¡Ándale!" They were cutting through the cattle on their horses, swinging their lassoes in the air to rope out the steers. My *tío* Chaco threw his saddle up on his horse, Canelo, and joined them. We kids clapped and whistled. Sometimes we helped my father or my *tíos*. We brought them rope or a fresh horse or something to drink.

That night we boys got to eat with the *vaqueros* and sit by the fire and listen to them play their guitars and sing their *rancheras*. We got to hear their exciting stories and their bragging and their bad words. When my father came over to Junior and me I thought he was going to tell us to go in to bed, but instead he said, "Tomorrow I want you boys to help with the branding." Junior had helped since he was eleven, but it was the first time my father had ever asked me.

"Tomorrow I have school," I said.

"School!" said Junior. "Monchi, you *burro*, don't you understand? You get to help with the branding!"

"He doesn't want to lose the Perfect Attendance," said Victor.

"The Perfect Attendance!" said Junior. "Monchi, you are crazier than a goat. You are a Ramírez. We are a family of *vaqueros*. Roundup is more important than the Perfect Attendance."

I knew Junior was right, but I touched the empty hole of my silver-dollar buckle and I sighed. *Adiós*, Perfect Attendance.

For two exciting days Junior and I helped with the roundup. First the *vaqueros* lassoed the calves and wrestled them down to the ground. Then Junior and I held them while my father and my *tío* Enrique branded them and cut the ears and gave them the shot.

¡Qué barullo! The red-hot irons were smoking, and the burned hair was stinking. The calves were fighting and bawling like giant babies. They were much heavier than Junior and me. It was hard work and dangerous to hold them down. I got dust in my eyes and in my nose, but I didn't care.

Sunday morning the *vaqueros* sent Junior and me to get mesquite for the fire. When we came back we saw they had killed a cow and dug a big hole. They put the wood in the hole and lit it and put rocks on top. When the fire burned down, they put first the head of the cow, then a wet gunny sack,

then dirt. The rest of the cow they gave to the roundup cook to make the *barbacoa*.

After the work of the roundup was over, we made the *fiesta*! First was a race for the kids. We had to ride as fast as we could to the chuck wagon, take an orange, and ride back again. Junior won on Pinto. He got a big jar of candies and gave some to all of us. Last came Victor on his little *burro*. All that day we had races and roping contests.

That night we had a big *barbacoa*. The kids got cold soda pops. When the music started, all the *vaqueros* wanted to dance with Natalia. The one they call Chapo asked her to be his *novia*, but Natalia told him she doesn't want to get married. She wants to go to high school.

Monday morning when we left for school, the *vaqueros* were packing their bedrolls. We waved and hollered from our bus, "¡Adiós! ¡Adiós! ¡Hasta la vista!"

Of course Victor *El Chismoso* had told Miss Byers why I wasn't in school on Friday,

and she had marked me absent.

"Maybe someday you will stop being such a big *chismoso*," I told Victor. "Maybe someday you will even be a *vaquero*, like the other men of the Ramírez family."

40

Issue Number Nine   May 10, 1939

COYOTE NEWS

¡Hasta la vista!

Stories and Pictures by the Students of Coyote School, Pima County, Arizona

Adios Coyote School! *Lalo Natalia* *Good-bye, everybody! Thank you, Miss Byers!*

by Lalo Lopez

Eduardo (Lalo) and Natalia Graduate!

Lalo and I have passed the Eighth Grade Standard Achievement Test! I am happy to graduate and I am excited about high school, but I will miss my teacher and all the kids at my dear Coyote School...Natalia Ramirez, Grade 8

I Lose the Perfect Attendance

I was absent from school to help with the roundup. It was very exciting, but now it is over and I am feeling sad. The vaqueros are gone and I will not get a silver dollar for my buckle....Monchi Ramirez, Grade 4

The Perfect Attendance Report

The only one who still has perfect attendance is Victor. Even Miss Byers has been absent, because when it was roundup on her ranch a big calf stepped on her foot. We had Miss Elias for 3 days. Miss Byers had to pay her 5 dollars a day to take her place.....Gilbert Perez, Grade 6

Please forgive me, Miss Byers

300 pounds

By Rosie García

A Visit to the Boston Beans

Mr. and Mrs. Bean invited my family to visit them this summer in Boston. Boston is Back East. It is even bigger than Tucson. No other kid at Coyote School has ever gone that far away!.............Billy Mills, Grade 3

Earrings

My daddy is getting married. Joey and I will get a new mother and 4 new brothers. Laura is nice and she can cook, but the best part is she has pierced ears and now I will get to have them too!....Cynthia Brown, Grade 2

Last Issue for the School Year

This is the last issue before the summer vacation. I am saving all my Coyote News newspapers so that someday I can show my children all the swell and exciting things we did at Coyote School...........Rosie Garcia, Grade 3

THE LAST DAY OF SCHOOL

On the last day of school Miss Byers gave us a *fiesta* with cupcakes and candies and Cracker Jacks and soda pops. We got to listen to Mexican music on her radio. I didn't have to dance with Natalia. I got to dance with Rosie.

Then Miss Byers turned off the radio and stood in the front of the room between President Roosevelt and *Señor Grandote*. She called Natalia and Lalo up to the front and told them how proud we were that they were graduates of Coyote School, and how much we would miss them. We all clapped and whistled.

Next, Miss Byers gave Edelia a paper and said, "Please read what it says, Edelia."

Edelia read: "Edelia Ortiz has been promoted to Grade Two." Miss Byers had to help her to read "promoted," but we all clapped and cheered anyway. Edelia looked very happy and proud.

Ramón Ernesto Ramírez."

"*Me?*" I said.

All the kids were clapping and whistling. I just sat there.

"Go up to the front, you *burro*," Natalia said and gave me a push.

Miss Byers smiled and shook my hand. "Congratulations, Monchi," she said, and then she gave me the award.

¡Ay caramba! The *Coyote News* Writing Award was a shiny silver dollar!

"Oh thank you, Miss Byers!" I said. "*¡Gracias!*" I was so surprised and happy. I pushed the silver dollar into the round hole on my buckle. It fit perfectly!

"*¡Muy hermosa!*" Miss Byers said.

She was right. It was very beautiful.

Then Miss Byers asked Victor to come to the front of the room, and I knew what that meant. I didn't want to listen when she said how good it was that he had not missed a day of school, and I didn't want to look when she gave him the silver dollar. I knew I should be happy that Victor won the Perfect Attendance, but I was not.

"And now, boys and girls," Miss Byers said, "it's time for the next award."

"What next award?" we asked.

"The *Coyote News* Writing Award for the student who has contributed most to *Coyote News* by writing his own stories and by helping others write theirs. The winner of the *Coyote News* Writing Award is

Spanish Words in the Story (and How to Pronounce Them)

americano (AH-mair-ee-CAHN-oh)—
American

ándale (AHN-dah-lay)—come on; hurry up

¡ay caramba! (EYE car-RAHM-bah)—oh boy!

barbacoa (bar-bah-KOH-ah)—barbecue

barullo (bah-ROO-yoe)—noise, racket

bolas (BOWL-ahs)—balls of raw dough

broncos (BRAHNK-ohs)—unbroken horses

burro (BOOR-row)—donkey, stupid

cabestros (kah-BESS-troes)—horsehair
ropes, halters

camisas (kah-MEE-sahs)—shirts

campo (KAHM-poe)—playing field

carne (CAR-nay)—meat

cerro (SAIR-roe)—hill

chiles (CHEE-less)—chile peppers

chismoso (cheese-MOE-soe)—tattletale

chúcata (CHEW-kah-tah)—mesquite sap

comal (koh-MAHL)—griddle

comida (koh-MEE-dah)—meal

con (cone)—with

¡dále! (DAH-lay)—hit it!

de (day)—of

del (dell)—of the

día (DEE-ah)—day

feliz (fay-LEASE)—happy

fiesta (fee-ESS-tah)—party, celebration

frijoles (free-HOE-less)—beans

gracias (GRAHS-see-ahs)—thank you

grandote (grahn-DOE-tay)—great big, huge

hasta la vista (AH-stah lah VEE-stah)—
see you

hermosa (air-MOE-sah)—beautiful

hoja (OH-hah)—cornhusk

la (lah)—the

loco, un loco (oon LOW-coe)—crazy,
a crazy person

los (lohs)—the

magnífico (mahg-NEE-fee-koe)—great

masa (MAH-sah)—dough

mascada (mas-KAH-dah)—scarf

menudo (men-OO-doe)—tripe soup

mi'jo (MEE-hoe)—my son, sonny

mira (MEER-ah)—look

moscas (MOES-cahs)—flies

muertos (moo-AIR-toes)—dead

muy (mooey)—very

nacimiento (nah-see-mee-EN-toe)—
nativity scene

Navidad (nahv-ee-DAHD)—Christmas

Nochebuena (NO-chay-BUAY-nah)—
Christmas Eve

novia (NOVE-ee-ah)—girlfriend

olla (OY-yah)—clay pot

pan (pahn)—bread

perezoso (pair-eh-ZO-soe)—lazy

piñata (peen-YAH-tah)—clay pot (*olla*)
filled with treats

pobrecito (pobe-ray-SEE-toe)—poor little
thing

qué (kaye)—what, how

queso (KAYE-sew)—cheese

ramada (rah-MAH-dah)—shelter

rancheras (rahn-CHAIR-ahs)—Mexican
folk songs

rancho (RAHN-choe)—ranch

san (sahn)—saint

sartas (SAR-tahs)—strings of chile peppers

seca (SAY-kah)—dry

señor (sin-YORE)—Mr.

sol (sole)—sun

tamales (tah-MAH-less)—steamed
filled dough

tía (TEE-ah)—aunt

tío (TEE-oh)—uncle

todos (TOE-dose)—all

tonta (TONE-tah)—silly

tortillas (tor-TEE-yahs)—flat Mexican bread

vaqueros (bah-CARE-rose)—cowboys

Coyote School

Billy   Monchi   Lalo   Frankie   Natalia